PEANUT BUTTER & ~~JELLY~~ BRAINS

A ZOMBIE CULINARY TALE

Words by

Joe McGee

Pictures by

Charles Santoso

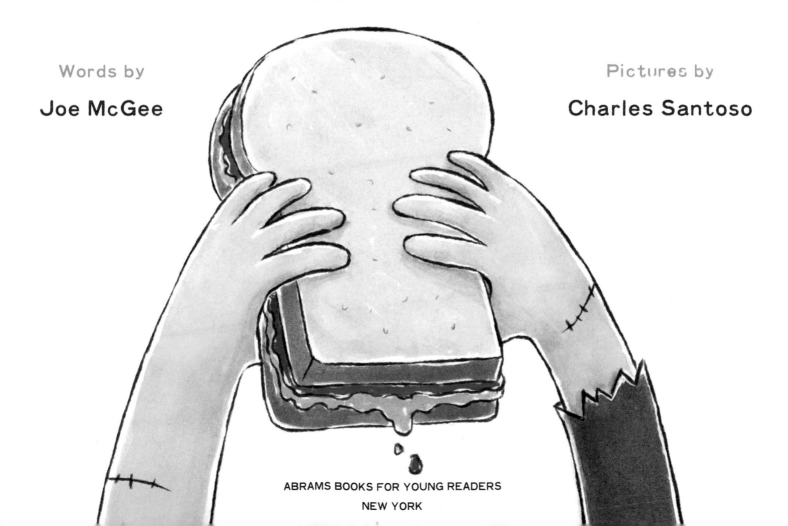

ABRAMS BOOKS FOR YOUNG READERS

NEW YORK

The illustrations in this book were made with
pen and ink and then colored with watercolor.

Library of Congress Cataloging-in-Publication Data

McGee, Joe, 1972-
Peanut butter and brains / words by Joe McGee ; pictures by Charles Santoso.
pages cm
Summary: Unlike the other zombies in Quirkville, Reginald would rather eat a peanut butter
and jelly sandwich than brains, but getting his hands on one—and keeping the other
zombies' hands off the girl who is carrying the sandwich—will not be easy.
ISBN 978-1-4197-1247-0
[1. Zombies—Fiction. 2. Food habits—Fiction. 3. Humorous stories.]
I. Santoso, Charles, illustrator. II. Title.
PZ7.1.M435Pe 2015
[E]—dc23
2014041420

Text copyright © 2015 Joe McGee
Illustrations copyright © 2015 Charles Santoso
Book design by Chad W. Beckerman

Printed and bound in China
10 9 8 7 6 5 4 3 2 1

Abrams Books for Young Readers are available at
special discounts when purchased in quantity for
premiums and promotions as well as fundraising
or educational use. Special editions can also be
created to specification. For details, contact
specialsales@abramsbooks.com or the address below.

ABRAMS
THE ART OF BOOKS SINCE 1949
115 West 18th Street
New York, NY 10011
www.abramsbooks.com

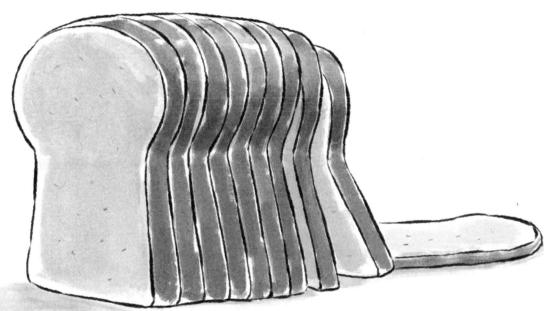

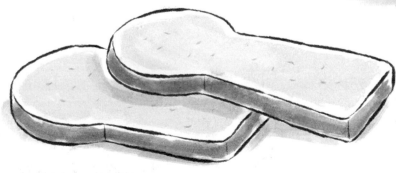

Reginald was not like the other zombies.

The other zombies wanted brains for breakfast, lunch, and dinner. But not Reginald.

All Reginald wanted was a peanut butter and jelly sandwich.

"BRAINSSSSS," moaned the zombie horde, shuffling through the streets of Quirkville. Wherever the zombies went, people ran, screaming in fear. Nobody wanted their brains eaten. Not for breakfast, not for lunch, not even for dinner.

Reginald didn't shuffle with them. His stomach rumbled and growled, and all he could do was dream about a peanut butter and jelly sandwich. "Sweet jelly . . . ," moaned Reginald. "Sticky peanut butter . . ."

"NO BRAI

the other zombies asked.

"No brains," said Reginald. "Peanut butter and jelly."
The other zombies shook their heads.

"If you tried peanut butter and jelly," said Reginald,
"you'd never want brains again."

But the zombies
just shambled off.

Reginald went to the corner cafe and tried to order a sandwich,
but the man behind the counter shook his head and pointed to a sign.

He tried the school cafeteria, but the lunch lady slapped a hunk of meat loaf on his tray instead.

It looked an awful lot like brains.

Reginald even tried Oscar's Grocery. But when Oscar rang up the loaf of bread, the peanut butter, and the strawberry jelly, Reginald couldn't pay.

"Sorry," said Oscar. "Paying customers only."

Reginald left the store
and his groceries behind.

Across the street stood little Abigail Zink, the smartest girl in Quirkville. She carried a lunch bag in her hand.

Reginald recognized the familiar jelly stain that was seeping through the paper bag.

"PEANUT BUTTER AND JELLYYYYY,"

he moaned.

The zombie horde shuffled and shambled around the corner.

"BRAINSSSSS,"

they moaned, licking their lips at the sight of little Abigail Zink.

The townspeople froze in their tracks, including the mayor and his prancing poodle.

Suddenly, little Abigail Zink dropped the bag holding her peanut butter and jelly sandwich.

Reginald lurched forward and seized it.

He raised the jelly-stained bag to his lips. He could practically taste the delicious sticky peanut butter and sweet strawberry jelly.

Little Abigail Zink let out a shriek, the mayor's poodle yipped and yapped, and the townspeople all screamed,

"AHHHHH!"

If the other zombies could just
smell the peanut butter, Reginald
thought. If they could just *taste*
the sweet jelly . . .

"BRAINS!"

cried Reginald, holding up the
peanut butter and jelly sandwich.

"BRAINSSSSS," moaned the zombies, reaching for the sandwich.

Reginald threw it into the crowd of drooling zombies.

When the zombies tore into the peanut butter and jelly sandwich, their eyes lit up. "Not brains?" they said, licking their lips. "Yummy! Better than brains!"

The zombies rubbed their bellies, and the townspeople smiled.

"Why, they're just hungry," declared the mayor. "And peanut butter and jelly does the trick!"

Peanut butter and jelly *did* do the trick.

The zombies no longer wanted brains, and the townspeople were no longer afraid of the zombies. Soon, the zombies were a regular part of Quirkville.

They collected the garbage, walked dogs, and swept the streets.

They were happy to help and even happier to be paid in peanut butter and jelly sandwiches.

But Reginald still wasn't like the other zombies . . .

. . . because while they were enjoying their peanut butter and jelly sandwiches, Reginald had moved on to . . .

PIZZA.

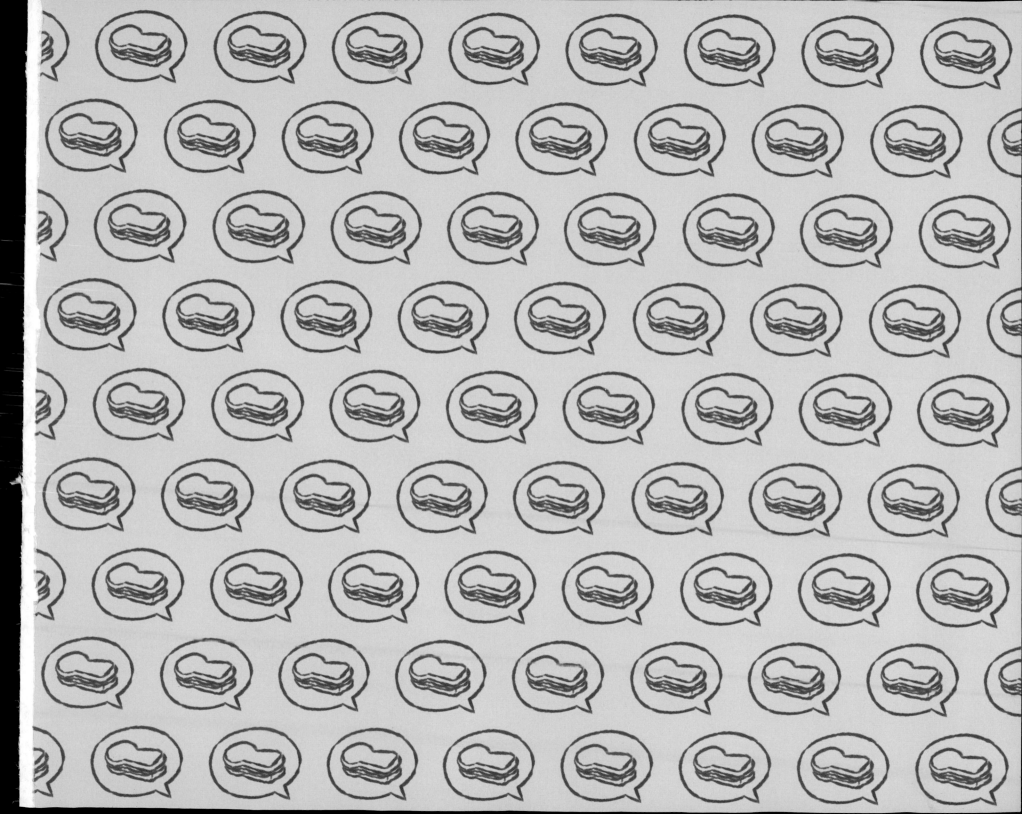

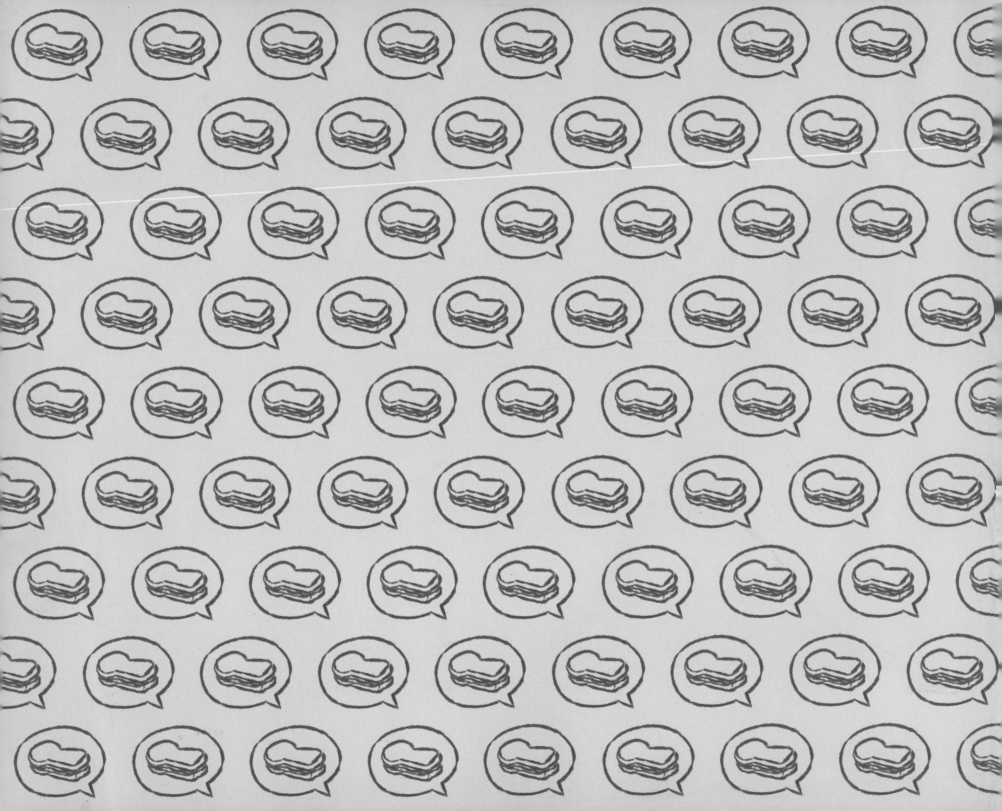